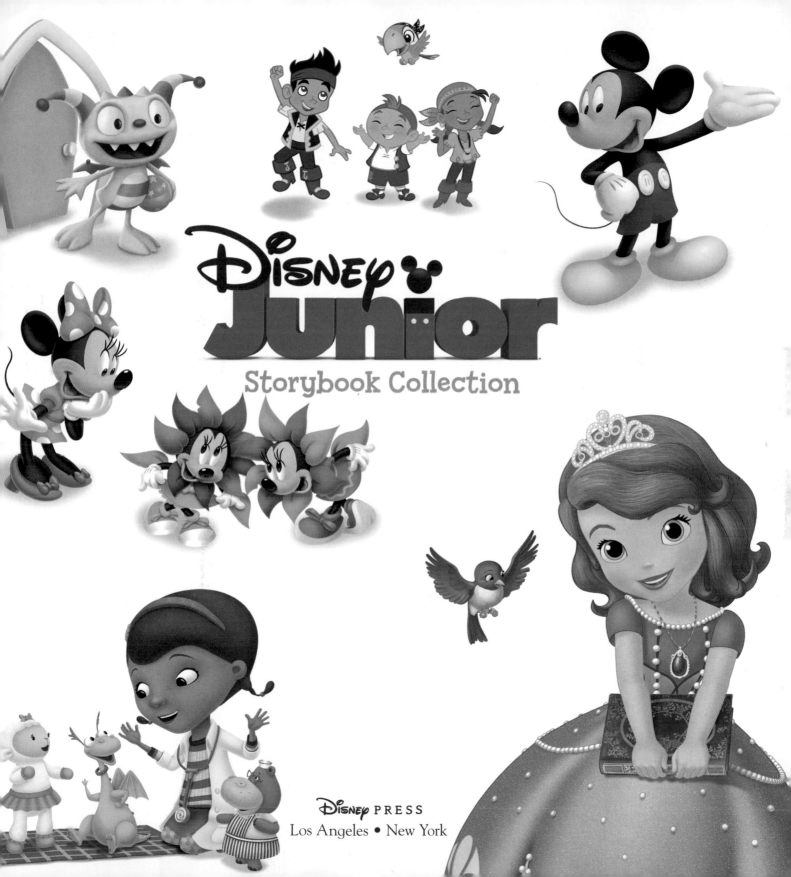

Disney Junior

Storybook Collection

Disney PRESS

Los Angeles • New York

CONTENTS

The Princess Test

At Royal Prep, it's almost time for dance class to begin. Sofia and the other princesses are stretching when Flora, Fauna, and Merryweather float in.

"May I have your attention, please?" Flora says. "We won't be having dance class today. Instead, you'll be preparing for a very important test."

"The Princess Test!" Merryweather adds.

Sofia has no idea what a princess test might be. Before she can ask, Fauna explains, "The Princess Test is your chance to show us everything you've learned about being a true princess."

"Everything?" Princess Jun exclaims. "But we've learned so much!"

The fairies tell them that the test will take place in the ballroom right after school. "Good luck, everyone!" Fauna says as the fairies flutter out.

Sofia, Amber, Jun, and Hildegard go to the library to prepare for the Princess Test. The librarian, Mrs. Higgins, finds them some books to study and wishes them luck.

Sofia pages through a book. "Do they really expect us to know all these things?" she wonders. "Banquet Manners? Tea Party Conversation?"

The other princesses don't seem worried. "You'll do fine, Sofia," Jun says.

"But I haven't been a princess very long," Sofia reminds the others. "There's so much I don't know."

"Just make sure your gown looks gorgeous—like mine—and you'll do fine," Amber assures her. "That's the most important thing to know about being a princess."

Hildegard flips open her fan. "But proper fan fluttering is a must, too."

Sofia hopes she can remember everything they're telling her. Especially since it's almost time for the test to start!

"You go ahead," Sofia says as the others head for the ballroom. "I want to make sure my dress looks perfect."

The other princesses pass Mrs. Higgins. "Princess Amber!" the librarian calls. "Can you help me?"

"I wish I could, Mrs. Higgins," Amber replies. "But the Princess Test is about to start."

"I understand, dear," Mrs. Higgins says. She asks Jun and Hildegard for help, too. But both girls apologize and hurry past.

Finally, Sofia comes along. "What's the matter, Mrs. Higgins?" she asks.

"Oh, thank you for stopping!" the librarian cries. "I have to bring these books home, but my wheelbarrow broke and I can't carry them myself. Will you help me? I don't live far—just down the path a wee bit."

"Umm . . ." Sofia glances toward the ballroom, not sure what to do.

Mrs. Higgins smiles hopefully. Sofia sighs and smiles back.

"Of course I'll help you," she says. She's sure she still has enough time before the Princess Test starts.

The two of them gather the books and head off down the path. Before long, Mrs. Higgins points ahead.

"My cottage is just across this bridge—oh, huckleberry!" she exclaims. A tree has fallen on the footbridge!

"How are we going to get to your cottage?" Sofia wonders.

"Well, there's another way," Mrs. Higgins says. "But it'll take a bit longer."

Sofia gulps. "Longer? But that might make me late for the Princess Test."

"I understand if you need to go back," Mrs. Higgins says. "I'll be okay on my own."

Sofia thinks about it. Then she shakes her head. "I can't let you carry all these heavy books yourself, Mrs. Higgins. Lead the way."

Sofia and Mrs. Higgins walk for a while. "Is your cottage far from here?" Sofia asks.

"Not really," Mrs. Higgins says cheerfully. "I'll draw you a map."

She scribbles in the dirt with a stick. "Um, maybe we should keep going, Mrs. Higgins?" Sofia suggests.

"Yes, indeed." Mrs. Higgins gestures toward a narrow pass between two boulders. "After you, my dear!" Sofia steps forward. Then she stops.

"I'm so sorry," she says. "A proper princess would say 'After you!'"

Mrs. Higgins smiles. "You are a proper princess."

"Not really." Sofia sighs. "I wasn't born a princess, so sometimes I feel like I have to keep proving I belong."

Mrs. Higgins pats her shoulder. "From what I've seen, Sofia, I think you make a wonderful princess."

Sofia and Mrs. Higgins continue on their way. Soon they reach a rushing stream.

"Where's the bridge?" Sofia asks.

Mrs. Higgins chuckles. "We don't need a bridge. We can just walk across the rocks."

Just then Sofia hears the school bell ring in the distance. "Oh, no," she cries. "The Princess Test is starting! I'd better hurry."

"Follow me." Mrs. Higgins skips across the stream on the rocks. Sofia follows, but the rocks are slippery, and her fan flies into the water!

"My fan!" Sofia cries, watching the water swirl her fan away. "Hildegard said the fan is a really important part of the Princess Test. Now I lost it and I'm late. What am I going to do?"

Mrs. Higgins offers again to let Sofia turn back. But Sofia knows the books are too heavy for one person.

"I'm not leaving until we get you home," she says. "Besides, my gown still looks nice. My sister said that's the most important part of the test."

"Did she?" Mrs. Higgins says. "My cottage is just through those trees. . . ."

Soon Sofia spots the cottage. It's not far—but the path passes right through a muddy bog!

Once again, Mrs. Higgins offers to let Sofia turn back. But Sofia has a better idea. She holds up the edge of her gown to keep it clean.

There's just one problem—the mud is slippery. Halfway across, Mrs. Higgins slips and falls.

"I've got you!" Sofia cries, trying to catch her.

They both end up falling in the mud. Sofia's gown is filthy!

"I'm so sorry, Sofia," Mrs. Higgins says. "But I couldn't have made it home without you. Thank you."

Mrs. Higgins's words make Sofia feel better. "You're welcome," she says. "I may not have made it to the Princess Test, but at least we got you home."

"Don't give up on that test yet," Mrs. Higgins says. "Come this way. . . ."

She leads Sofia into her cottage—which transforms into the Royal Prep ballroom! All the other princesses are there, along with Flora and Merryweather.

"Sofia!" Amber exclaims. "Where'd you come from? And what happened to your dress?"

Sofia is confused—especially when she sees a second Mrs. Higgins standing nearby! The first Mrs. Higgins pulls out a wand and transforms into Fauna.

"I used magic to make myself look like Mrs. Higgins," Fauna explains. "It was all part of the Princess Test! One of the most important things about being a princess is kindness. A true princess always helps a person in need."

Flora nods. "Even if it means giving up something very important to you."

Amber and the other princesses all end up doing well on the Princess Test. The fairies reward them with sparkly silver stars.

But Sofia was the only one who stopped to help Mrs. Higgins, so she wins a special gold trophy.

"Can I hold it?" Amber asks eagerly.

"Oh, Amber!" Sofia giggles, glad to know that she really does belong!

JAKE SAVES BUCKY

It's bedtime on the *Jolly Roger*, and Captain Hook wants Smee to read him a story. Smee finds an old scroll. "Here's one I've never seen before!" he says.

The scroll says that Jake's ship, Bucky, has to race against Hook's *Jolly Roger* the very next day. And, if Hook wins, he gets to keep Bucky as his prize!

When no one is looking, Hook tears off a piece of the scroll and stuffs it into his pocket.

Now, Captain Hook is sure he will win the race!

The next morning, Jake
and his crew are playing
Pirate Bop Beach Ball with Bucky.

Bucky plays by using his sail boom like a bat.

"Yo-ho, watch the beach ball go!" exclaims Jake.

Oops! Bucky hits it a little too hard and the ball goes flying
over the railing.

Cubby goes to get it, but Hook snags it first.

Hook climbs aboard Bucky and hands the scroll to Jake.

"It says here Bucky has to race the *Jolly Roger* today. And if
he loses, Hook gets to take Bucky!" reads Jake.

That doesn't sound fair to Jake and
his crew.

"According to the Never Land
Pirate Code of Rules, you have
no choice!" snickers Hook.

Jake and the crew get ready, but Cubby is worried. "Um, Jake, what if we lose the race? We can't give up Bucky!" he cries.

"Cubby, we're not going to lose," replies Jake. "We're gonna win. Yo-ho! Now let's go to the starting line!"

The race starts at Shipwreck Beach. First the crews will race to Mermaid Lagoon. There, they'll have to solve a riddle to move to the next stop. Another riddle at the second stop will lead them to the end of the race.

With Bucky at stake, there is no way Hook will play fair. As soon as the race starts, he unleashes one of his fancy new gizmos—the Colossal Coconut Cannon! *BOOOMMM!*

Coconuts rain down on Bucky! Cubby and Izzy duck. "Aw, coconuts!" Cubby shouts.

Bucky slows down and waits for the next barrage. *BOOOMMM!* Then he uses his hatches and booms to knock all the coconuts back to the *Jolly Roger*! "Yo-ho!" exclaims Jake. "Bucky's playing Pirate Bop Beach Ball!"

Hook and his men run for cover. And with no one at the wheel, the *Jolly Roger* comes to a complete standstill.

Bucky zooms by and gets to Mermaid Lagoon first!

Jake reads the first riddle: "Find a fish that's not a fish."

The crew quickly spreads out to search. Soon Jake spots Sandy the Starfish. "Check it out, mates! Sandy's got the word 'fish' in his name."

"That makes him a fish that's not a fish!" exclaims Izzy.

Jake and the crew head to their next stop—Skull Rock.

Before long, the *Jolly Roger* makes it to Mermaid Lagoon, and Hook and his scallywags set out to solve the first riddle.

Captain Hook stomps around, almost stepping on Sandy the Starfish!

"Cap'n! That's it!" shouts Smee. "This starfish is the 'fish that's not a fish'!"

Now the *Jolly Roger* can head for Skull Rock.

Through his spyglass, Hook sees that Jake has a big lead. "Behold me newest trick—the Mighty Captain Hook Grappling Hook," he snarls.

Hook pulls a lever to launch a huge hook tied to an anchor. The grappling hook soars through the air and latches on to Bucky. When the anchor drops into the water, Jake's ship is dead in the water!

But Hook isn't done. "Engage the Pirate Propeller!" he commands. A large propeller appears, and the *Jolly Roger* surges ahead.

Hook waves as he speeds past Bucky. "See you later!"

Finally, Jake is able to pry the hook off Bucky.

Bucky and the Never Land pirates hurry toward the next stop, but Hook is far, far ahead and has already reached Skull Rock!

Hook has just one riddle left to solve: "Find an island shaped like a bird." He scans the horizon with his spyglass and spies Eagle Island. "Glory be! Move it, Smee! I'm about to win!" he shouts.

When Bucky lands at Skull Rock, Skully instantly knows the answer to the riddle. "I've got this one, mateys. It's Eagle Island!"

But Jake's crew is too late. Captain Hook beats them to Eagle Island!

"I win! I win the Great Never Sea Race! Bucky is mine, all mine!" gushes Hook.

Jake can't believe it. "This can't be happening," he says.

Smee hands Jake the Pirate Code of Rules scroll. "I'm sorry, Jake. But I'm afraid pirates' rules are pirates' rules."

Hook's crew ties Bucky
to the *Jolly Roger*. Then
Jake, Izzy, and Cubby sadly
say good-bye to their friend.
Izzy sprinkles everyone with
Pixie Dust, and the crew flies
home to Pirate Island.

That night, Bucky rings his bell over and over. Hook orders
Sharky and Bones to stop the ringing. But Bucky slams his doors
and rolls a barrel across his deck
to scare them off. It works!
Sharky and Bones race
back to the *Jolly Roger*
as fast as they can. "I
tells ya, Bones, this ship
be haunted."

Back home, the Never Land pirates need help, and Jake knows who to call—Peter Pan! Using the Lunar Lantern to shine his picture on the moon, Jake calls, "Cock-a-doodle-doo, Peter Pan, we need you!" Peter Pan comes right away.

Jake tells Peter what happened and shows him the scroll.

"Hmm. There seems to be a piece of the scroll missing," says Peter.

"Maybe there's more to the rules than what Hook showed us! Quick, to the *Jolly Roger*!" exclaims Jake.

Peter Pan and the crew quickly fly to the *Jolly Roger* to search for the missing piece. They look *absolutely everywhere*. Finally, Peter looks in the pocket of Hook's nightshirt, and he finds it!

The friends read the missing piece and discover they have one last chance to get Bucky back! They have to go to the Island of Bell and bring back the Great Golden Bell before sunrise.

But there is also a warning: *Pirates beware! A mighty dragon lives on the Island of Bell—and he doesn't like visitors!*

Peter and the Never Land pirates head off and soon land on the windy, fiery Island of Bell. With his spyglass, Jake spots something golden hanging from a giant tree in the next valley. It's the Great Golden Bell!

But to get to the bell, the friends have to face a blustery wind and hike across a field of hot lava!

All of a sudden, the dragon appears—roaring and breathing fire!

Peter Pan has a plan. "Jake, you and I will distract old Furnace Face. Cubby, Izzy, Skully—you run ahead and grab the Great Golden Bell."

Peter and Jake soon have the dragon twisting, turning, and chasing his own tail! Meanwhile, Cubby, Izzy, and Skully run to the giant tree and find the golden bell.

Just then, Jake and Peter Pan return to help.

"This old dinger sure is heavy!" says Peter Pan.

"A little bit of Pixie Dust will help us get it back to Bucky!" Izzy says.

Peter and the crew sail over to the *Jolly Roger* just before dawn.

A surprised Hook asks, "Peter Pan! What are you doing here?"

Jake shows Hook the repaired scroll. "It says we can rescue Bucky by bringing the Great Golden Bell back before sunrise. And we did it!" he says.

"BARNACLES!" grumbles Captain Hook.

Everyone rushes to tell Bucky the good news.

"We did it! We saved you from Hook!" cheers Jake.

Izzy smiles. "We'll never let you down, Bucky. Never ever!"

Then they all wave good-bye to Peter Pan and thank him for his help.

"That's what best mates do!" Peter Pan replies.
"Cock-a-doodle-doo!"

Disney
MICKEY MOUSE CLUBHOUSE
MICKEY & DONALD HAVE A FARM

There's something brand new at the Clubhouse. Mickey can't wait to share it with everybody.

"I hope my new clothes don't give away my big surprise!" says Mickey. "But first, we'll get our Mouseketools!"

"We've got a fishing pole, the Blimpy Blazer for floatin' and flyin', a soft blanket—comfy!—and the Mystery Mouseketool!"

42

Suddenly, Donald and Pluto pull Mickey into the Anywhere Area. "Goofy's on the move!" Donald cries. "And we've got to stop him!"

"Whoa, ya tricky little tractor!" yells Goofy. "Help! I don't know how to stop this runaway clickety-clack tractor!"

Donald throws his lasso over the tractor's red STOP lever and pulls. It works! The tractor comes to a halt. "Sorry I goofed up," says Goofy.

"That's okay, Goof. You took us right where I wanted to go!" Mickey says. "Welcome to the Clubhouse Farm!"

Mickey and Donald grow fruits and veggies on the farm. They raise animals, too! The Clubhouse Farm is a very busy place.

Oh, Mickey 'n' Donald have a farm,
Meeska, Mouseke-doo!
And on our farm we have lots of fun,
Meeska, Mouseke-doo!

Mickey explains, "Everyone helps out at the Clubhouse Farm."

"We're picking lots of apples today," says Daisy. "They're *deeee-lish*!"

"And the cows are making sure we have plenty of milk, too!" adds Minnie.

All of a sudden, a mighty wind begins to blow. "Whoa!" shouts Mickey. "Hold on to your hats, everybody!"

Everything is being blown around—even the animals!

"That wind could wreck the farm," warns Mickey.

Mickey has to shout to be heard over the whooshing wind.

But there is another sound, too—an unusual whirring sound.

"Come on, guys," calls Mickey. "Let's hop on the clickety-clack tractor and find out what's making that strange sound!"

"Gawrsh!" says Goofy. "It's a giant windy-mill!"

"Farmer Pete! What's going on?" asks Mickey.

"Sorry for all the wind," says Pete. "I was using my new windmill to keep the bugs away from my prize petunias."

"Why don't you turn the windy-mill off?" yells Goofy.

Farmer Pete shrugs. "I don't know which lever to pull."

Goofy says, "I remember that red means STOP."

"Then let's try it," says Mickey.

Goofy grabs the red lever and pulls.

"The windmill stopped!" Mickey cheers.

"Thanks, everybody," calls Farmer Pete.

Back at the farm, something is plainly wrong.

"Golly," says Goofy. "All the animals are missing! They must have blown away like birdies."

"Come on," says Mickey. "Let's find the animals."

Just then, Minnie and Daisy point up. The pony is sitting on top of the silo!

"We've got to help," says Goofy. "If only she could fly."

"Oh, Toodles!" Mickey calls.

Which Mouseketool will help the pony float to the ground? Right! The Blimpy Blazer!

"All right! We got the pony down safely," says Mickey.

Suddenly, the friends hear another sound. *Oink, oink, oink!*

It's the piggies! The cluck-cluck chicken coop sheltered them from the wind. But now the piggies are ready to come down.

"Uh-oh," says Mickey. "The piggies need a safe place to land!"

Mickey and his friends call, "Oh, Toodles!"

Toodles appears in a jiffy with the perfect Mouseketool— a nice, soft blanket!

Donald and Goofy hold the blanket tight as the piggies glide down the twisty slide. One, two, three little piggies!

Goofy and Donald help the horsey and piggies into the clickety-clack tractor's wagon.

On the way back to the barn, Mickey hears Farmer Clarabelle. "Oh, cluck-cluck chickens, where can you be?" she cries.

Mickey has an idea. "Your chickens love to sing," he says. "Let's all sing a song together. I bet the cluck-cluck chickens will come out and join in, too!"

"Oh, Mickey 'n' Donald have a farm,
Meeska, Mouseke-doo!
And on our farm we have cluck-cluck chickens,
Meeska, Mouseke-doo!"

Before long, Clarabelle's chickens come out of the tall grass.

Clarabelle is so happy. "Oh, thank you, Mickey!" she says.

Mickey smiles. "Aw, helping friends is what friends are for!"

53

Soon the friends see somebody else in need of help.

"Cowabunga!" says Goofy. "Mrs. Cow is stuck in that tire like a cork in a bottle!"

"We need a Mouseketool!" says Mickey. "Let's use the fishing pole to catch the tire!"

"Yeah!" says Goofy. "Then the tire will stop swinging!"

"And the cow, too!" Donald adds.

Donald catches the tire and holds it steady.

"Okeydoke, Mrs. Cow," Goofy says calmly. "Just wiggle yourself out and . . ."

Suddenly, Mrs. Cow pops free and lands right in Goofy's arms!

"Hot dog!" says Mickey. "Now it's back to the barn!"

Without warning—
BOOM!—a clap
of thunder surprises
everybody! Dark clouds
roll in.

"We need to blow
away these stormy
clouds," says Mickey.

"Oh, Toodles!" the gang calls.

The only tool left is the Mystery
Mouseketool. "It's Pete's windmill!"
exclaims Mickey.

"But that's what blew all the
animals away!" says Goofy.

"Yeah," says Mickey. "But
now we can blow the clouds away!"

Mickey tilts Pete's windmill to the sky. "Pull the lever that makes the windmill go," he says.

"Red means STOP, so it's not the red lever," Goofy says.

"But green means . . . GO!" shouts Donald.

The windmill's blast of air blows the storm away!

"Hot dog!" cries Mickey as he drives back to the barn.

The farm is saved!

"Oh, Mickey 'n' Donald have a farm,
Meeska, Mouseke-doo!
And everything's back the way it was,
Meeska, Mouseke-doo!"

Bronto Boo-Boos

"Pardon me, Miss Lambie, but would you care for a spot of tea?" asks Doc.

"A spot of tea would be most lovely!" giggles Lambie.

Doc hears running in the hallway. "Uh-oh, sounds like Donny is home from the arcade. I think you better go stuffed!"

"Hey, Doc! Where's Bronty's invite to the tea party?" jokes Donny.

Doc laughs. "Oh my, it must've gotten lost in the mail. Bronty is always welcome to join our tea parties."

"You and Bronty can sip tea later," Mom declares. "You're all sticky from the arcade. Time for a bath, young man!"

"You can play with Bronty while I'm gone," Donny tells Doc.

When Donny leaves the room, Doc's stethoscope starts to glow and the toys come to life. Bronty gallops around Doc's room.

"Whoa!" giggles Doc. "You sure like to stomp around."

Lambie politely tries to get Bronty's attention. "Would you like to join our tea party?"

"Ooooh, I sure would!" Bronty is so excited that he jumps up and down on the table, knocking over the teapot and cups.

"Hmmm, maybe tea party isn't the best game for you. Why don't we go outside to play?" Doc suggests.

Bronty is thrilled to play outdoors, where he has enough room to run around. He runs up to Stuffy, who's holding a ball.

"Ooh, can we play catch? Huh? Can we? Can we? *Puh-leeeeeze?*" begs Bronty.

As Stuffy throws the ball, Bronty races after it. Chilly and Squeakers jump out of the way to avoid being knocked down.

As the ball is thrown again, Bronty runs but doesn't watch where he's going. He sends Sir Kirby sailing into the air, steps on Ricardo Racecar, and makes Surfer Girl topple over!

"Like, careful there, dino dude!" mutters Surfer Girl.

Bronty feels bad. "Oops, sorry."

Surfer Girl tosses the ball and Bronty runs after it, this time trampling on top of Stuffy.

"Sorry," Bronty says again. "Now throw it. *Puh-leeeeze?* Throw it, c'mon, throw it!"

Stuffy tosses the ball but decides to take a break from playing. He's feeling a bit sore. He heads into Doc's clinic for a checkup.

Doc listens to Stuffy's heart and lungs with her stethoscope. "Where does it hurt?"

"Well . . . it only hurts here, here, here, here, and here." Stuffy points to his arm, his head, his tail, his tummy, and his left toe.

"Oh, sweet sugar lumps!" exclaims Hallie. "You've got a whole bushelful of boo-boos!"

"When did the ouches start?" asks Doc.

Stuffy thinks for a moment. "Well, it started when Surfer Girl threw the ball to Bronty, and he jumped up and landed on me."

Doc has a diagnosis. "Stuffy has a severe case of Bronto Boo-Boos. And I have the perfect treatment: a kiss and a cuddle!"

Hallie sees that Lambie, Squeakers, Surfer Girl, Sir Kirby, Ricardo, and Star Blazer Zero have entered the clinic. "Uh-oh, Doc. I think you have a heaping helping of new patients with Bronto Boo-Boos!"

The toys all line up to get a hug and a kiss from Doc. It's just the medicine they need to feel better!

To make sure the toys don't get Bronto Boo-Boos again, Doc has a talk with Bronty.

"I know you didn't mean to, but you hurt some of the toys today."

Bronty can't believe his ears. "*Me?!* I-I-I'm sorry, Doc. Aww, I hate being so big!"

"But being big is great!" says Doc. "You just have to be extra careful when you play with smaller toys.

"I have to do the same thing when I play with my little brother, Donny," Doc explains.

Bronty is surprised. "You have to be careful, too? Really?!"

"Really! People and toys come in all sizes. You're a big dinosaur—that's who you are and that's terrific! You just can't play so rough."

"Okay, Doc. I'll be careful and won't play rough anymore," Bronty promises.

Bronty finds his friends and apologizes for being so rough.

Lambie gives him a big cuddle. "It's okay, Bronty. We still love you!"

Bronty has an idea. "Hey, everyone, how about a ride on my back?"

Doc smiles. "See, Bronty? Being bigger can be pretty cool."

"In a *big* way!" agrees Bronty.

The Royal
Slumber Party

Sofia and Amber are having a royal sleepover tonight! "This is where we'll be sleeping," Amber says.

"The observatory? We get to sleep under the stars!" Sofia exclaims.

"It's a royal slumber party," Amber says. "Everything has to be *amazing*."

Sofia tells Amber that she invited her two best friends, Ruby and Jade. Amber is shocked. "You invited village girls? You're a princess now. You should only invite princesses to royal parties!"

"But Ruby and Jade are fun!" Sofia assures Amber. "You'll see."

Just then, the royal herald's trumpet sounds. "They're here!" Sofia cries.

Amber's friends, Princess Hildegard and Princess Clio, step out of their coaches. Behind them are Jade and Ruby, who jump from an oxcart.

"I can't believe we're here!" Jade exclaims, hugging Sofia.

It's time for the party to start! The princesses change into fancy nightgowns. Ruby and Jade giggle as they roll their hair in pinecone curlers—just like at home.

"We're at a royal sleepover!" they chant, grabbing Sofia to join their dance.

The other princesses stare at Ruby and Jade.

"What are they wearing?" Princess Hildegard says.

"What are they doing?" Princess Clio wonders.

Princess Amber frowns. "Are those pinecones?"

Ruby hears Amber and dances over. "Want some? We brought extras."

Amber grabs the pinecone and stomps over to Sofia. "Sofia! Pinecones are not part of an *amazing* royal slumber party."

Sofia is worried. She wants her new sister and her old friends to like each other.

"They can fit in," she says. "They just need a little help."

Sofia has a great idea. "How would you two like a royal makeover?" she asks her friends.

Ruby and Jade squeal with excitement!

Baileywick and Sofia's woodland friends help out. They fix the girls' hair and dress them in pretty gowns and tiaras.

Sofia makes her friends cover their eyes. Then she leads them to a mirror. "Open your eyes," she says.

Jade and Ruby gasp when they see themselves. "I'm a princess!" Ruby exclaims. "Me too!" calls Jade.

Next it's time for party activities.

First comes fan decorating. Ruby and Jade have fun. But their fans don't look very princessy.

Then the girls play a game of Pin the Tail on the Unicorn. "Ooh! Ooh!" Jade says. "Can I go first?" But Jade ends up nowhere near the unicorn!

After that, the girls watch a magic puppet show in the banquet hall. During the show, James, Sofia's brother, walks in to say hello.

"Prince James!" Jade and Ruby squeal, rushing toward him. They're thrilled to see the friendly prince!

Jade and Ruby are so excited to see James they accidentally knock over the chocolate milk fountain.

Oops! Chocolate milk splashes onto Amber's nightgown. She is furious!

"We're so, so, so sorry!" Ruby says to Amber.

"Yes, so sorry," Jade adds.

Amber walks off in a huff while Sofia shakes her head sadly.

Baileywick hurries Jade and Ruby away to get cleaned up.

Then James tells the girls it's time for dancing in the throne room.

"Let's go," Amber says. "Maybe we can enjoy five minutes of our party without Sofia's friends making a mess."

Now Sofia is even more worried! She goes off to find her friends.

"I want you both to fit in with the princesses," Sofia explains.

"We look just like them now, don't we?" Jade says.

"Yes," Sofia says. "But princesses don't talk so much, or laugh so loud, or make so many messes."

Jade frowns. "We were just having fun."

"We're sorry," Ruby adds quickly.
"We'll try to act more like Amber and the other princesses."

"Thank you!" sighs a relieved Sofia.
Now she is sure everyone will get along!

Sofia and her friends join the others in the throne room. But Ruby and Jade don't know how to waltz. All they can do is stand there and watch the princesses dance.

After a while, they tell Sofia they want to go home.

"But you're finally fitting in!" Sofia cries. "And you're not embarrassing me anymore!"

Her friends are hurt. "I'm sorry if we talk too much and laugh too loudly for your fancy new friends," says Jade. "Maybe we shouldn't be friends anymore!"

Ruby takes Jade's arm and together they rush out of the room.

"Don't worry about them," Hildegard tells Sofia. "You're with us now."

Sofia goes after her friends but finds her mother instead.

"I was trying to help Jade and Ruby fit in," she explains. "But I just made them feel bad."

"A true princess treats people with kindness, Sofia," Queen Miranda says gently. "If someone is your friend, you should like them for who they are and not who you or others want them to be." Sofia knows her mother is right.

Sofia runs outside and finds her friends just as they are about to leave. "I'm sorry about the way I acted," she says. "Please let me make it up to you. We can have our own slumber party—just the three of us!"

Jade and Ruby think for a moment and finally agree to stay.

Soon Sofia and her friends are in her room, having a great time. They laugh—loudly. They talk—a lot. They even make a little mess with feathers after a pillow fight. They roll pinecones in their hair and perch tiaras on top.

Meanwhile, Amber and her friends go back to the observatory.

"Finally, it's just us princesses," Amber says.

"This is just an *amazing* party," Hildegard agrees with a yawn.

There's a very long silence. Soon the princesses realize they are really, really bored.

"You know," Clio speaks up, "Sofia's friends were kind of fun to be with."

A moment later, Amber and her friends knock on Sofia's door.

"Do you have room for a few more princesses?" asks Amber.

Sofia looks at Jade and Ruby. "What do you think?"

"The more, the merrier," Ruby says with a smile.

Sofia and Amber end up having the perfect *amazing* sleepover with friends—both old and new!

Ahoy, Izzy!

"Want to play Ahoy 'n' Seek, mateys?" Jake asks.

Cubby scratches his head. "Ahoy 'n' Seek? What's that?"

"A game where someone hides while the others count to ten," says Izzy. "And when you find the person hiding, you shout, 'AHOY!'"

"That sounds like fun!" says Cubby.

"And the best part? When you're done counting, you blow this horn, which sounds just like the Never Sea whale," explains Jake.

BOW-OOOOH-GAH!

"What was that noise?"
says Captain Hook, aiming his
spyglass at Never Land. "Why,
it's an earsplitting, noisemaking
thingamajig! I must have it, Smee!"

snarls Hook. "Hurry, let's go ashore!"

"Ready, guys? I'm going to find the best hiding place ever,"
calls Izzy.

"Okay, we'll
start counting,"
says Cubby.

Cubby blows the
horn when they are
done counting.
*BOW-OOOOH-
GAH!*

Jake, Skully, and Cubby set out in search of Izzy's hiding place.

"Barnacles!" exclaims Cubby. "Where could she have gone?"

"Yo-ho, I spy a clue!" cries Jake. "See how there's a path of flattened grass here? She must have pushed the grass down when she walked on it."

"Over there, behind that tree!" shouts Cubby. "AHOY, IZZY!"
Jake giggles. "That's not Izzy. It's a flamingo!"
"Aw, coconuts!" says Cubby. "Now where should we look?"

"Say, me hearties," squawks Skully. "We haven't checked Bucky yet."

"Great idea, Skully!" says Jake.

The friends head toward their trusty ship.

With Jake and his crew busy looking for Izzy, Hook and Smee come ashore so Hook can nab the horn.

"Oh, my, Cap'n," says Smee. "Aren't those sea pups using the noisemaking thingamajig for their hiding game?"

Hook smiles slyly. "Do you see those puny pipsqueaks anywhere? Finders keepers!"

Meanwhile, on board Bucky, Jake thinks they've found Izzy.

"Look, sticking out of the closet—it's Izzy's bandana!"

They rush to the closet door. "AHOY, IZZY!"

"CRACKERS!" squawks Skully. "It's just a mop."

Just then, the sound of the Ahoy 'n' Seek horn bellows across the island.

BOW-OOOOH-GAH!

"Who could be blowing the horn?" asks Cubby.

Izzy darts out of her hiding spot. "I bet it's that sneaky snook Captain Hook!"

"Yo-ho, let's go get our horn!" shouts Jake.

"Barnacles and bilgewater! You blew it!" shouts Hook.

"Why, yes, Cap'n, I did," says a proud Smee.

"No, no, no, you blithering buffoon, I mean you blew our cover. Now those meddling swabs will know we've stolen their treasure."

Smee realizes his mistake. "Oh, dear!"

When Hook sees Jake and his crew coming toward him, he grabs the horn from Smee and starts to run.

"Well, blow me down!" Hook shouts frantically.

The playful Never Sea whale is more than happy to grant Captain Hook's wish.

He sprays a powerful blast of water right at the captain and blows him down!

"Yay-hey, no way!" Izzy springs into action when she sees the Ahoy 'n' Seek horn fly up into the air. "This looks like an emergency. I'd better use my Pixie Dust."

When Jake and Cubby see Izzy catch the horn in midair, they cheer, "AHOY, IZZY!"

"Well, that sure was a blast!" jokes Cubby.

"Stealing is never a good idea, Hook!" says Izzy.

"I guess your plan was all washed up from the start, Cap'n," says Smee.

"Playing Ahoy 'n' Seek was awesome!" says Cubby.

"Aye, and from the looks of it, the cap'n is still having a whale of a time!" squawks Skully.

Izzy blows the Ahoy 'n' Seek horn.

BOW-OOOOH-GAH!

Trouble Times Two

Minnie is hard at work in her busy Bow-tique.

"Oh, Cuckoo-Loca," says Minnie, "look what fantastic bows my new magic bejeweler makes!"

Suddenly, Minnie hears giggling!

"Who's making that noise?" she says.

"It's us, Aunt Minnie!" shout Millie and Melody.

Minnie greets her twin nieces. "Hello, Millie! Hello, Melody! How nice to have you visit the Bow-tique today!"

The girls begin running around the Bow-tique. Before long, they accidentally knock over several boxes of bows and beads!

"Can we help you make stuff today?" Millie asks.

"We promise to be extra good," adds Melody.

Cuckoo-Loca looks at the mess the girls have already made. "Famous last words," she says.

"How nice it will be to have two helpers today," says Minnie. "Why don't you unpack that box of ribbons for me?"

Just then, Daisy Duck rushes into the shop.

"Minnie!" she calls. "You're never going to believe it. . . ."

Oops-a-*Daisy*! She slips on the spilled beads and falls!

"Oh, Daisy!" cries Minnie. "Are you all right?"

"Never better," says Daisy. "Guess what famous movie superstar is on her way over to the Bow-tique right now?"

"Penelope Poodle?" guesses Minnie.

"Right!" cries Daisy. "I just got off the phone with her people. They made me promise that Penelope could shop here in total peace and quiet."

Suddenly, Millie and Melody zoom past.

"Hi, Daisy," the twins shout. "Sorry about the beads!"

Daisy looks at the girls and sighs. "Minnie, the twins are *not* total peace and quiet."

Minnie giggles. "Normally, that's true. But they promised to be extra good today."

Millie and Melody reach for some spools of colorful ribbon.

But down they go when the chair topples over! "Oops! Sorry, Aunt Minnie!" squeal the girls.

Just then, there's a huge commotion outside.

Penelope Poodle has arrived!

Excited fans and photographers crowd around the famous star.

"Look this way, Miss Poodle," shouts a photographer. "Can we get a smile?"

"Oh!" cries Daisy. "She's here!"

The glamorous Penelope Poodle glides through the door.

"Welcome to my Bow-tique," says Minnie.

"Hello," says Penelope. "You must help me. I'm accepting a Golden Bone award in less than an hour, and I need something fabulous to wear!"

Suddenly, Millie and Melody race past Penelope!

Penelope Poodle gasps. "I was promised I could shop in total peace and quiet."

Just then, Cuckoo-Loca pops up to snap a picture.

"Not now, Cuckoo-Loca," Daisy says firmly. "Minnie was just about to show Miss Poodle that one-of-a-kind thing she made."

Thinking fast, Minnie picks up the sparkly bow she made with her magic bejeweler and shows it to Penelope. "I call it the Glitterati," says Minnie.

Penelope Poodle is very impressed.

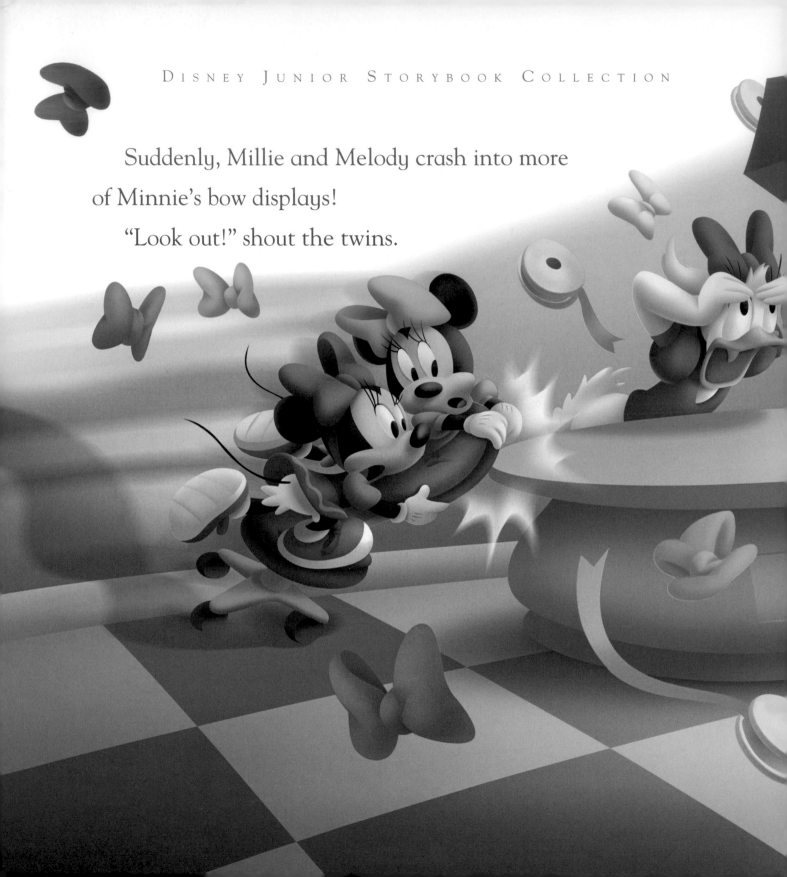

Suddenly, Millie and Melody crash into more
of Minnie's bow displays!
"Look out!" shout the twins.

They knock over racks of bows, boxes of ribbons, and even a can of paint.

The paint splatters everywhere!

Penelope Poodle has had enough. "I can see that coming here was a huge mistake."

"I am positive I can find you something gorgeous to wear," Minnie says, "if you'll just wait."

"Wait?" says Penelope. "I can't wait another moment! Oh, no! *Now* what are those little monsters doing to me?"

"Oh, they're not little monsters," says Minnie. "They're little *helpers*!"

She quickly uses the bejeweler to add bows and jewels to the twins' handiwork. "And I think they're on to something!"

Penelope Poodle looks in the mirror. "I look fabulous!" she says. "You're all *absolutely* brilliant!"

Everyone loves Penelope's new outfit.

"Miss Poodle!" calls a fan. "That's a fantastic look!"

"Who are you wearing?" asks a photographer.

Penelope smiles. "Who else? Minnie Mouse, of course!"

MICKEY MOUSE CLUBHOUSE

LOOK BEFORE YOU LEAP!

Mickey and Goofy are enjoying a quiet game of chess.

Just as Mickey is about to make a move, something soars through the window and lands right in the middle of the chessboard.

It is green. It has webbed feet. It says, *"Ribbit, ribbit."*

It is a frog—a *very* jumpy frog.

PLOP! The frog leaps right onto the silly switch.

Mickey tries to grab the frog, but it leaps right toward the . . . kitchen sink. *KERSPLASH!*

"You really should look before you leap!" Mickey says.

"What are we going to do about this big puddle?" Goofy asks.

"Oh, Toodles!" Mickey calls. "We need some Mouseketools— and we need them right away, please!"

"The mop is the right tool for this job," says Mickey.

Mickey's hard work makes Goofy hungry. He decides to make lunch. Just then, the frog takes a giant leap toward . . . Goofy's sandwich. *SQUISH!*

"Stop!" Mickey cries as Goofy is about to take a bite.

"You really *should* look before you leap," Goofy says to the frog, "and I should look before I bite!"

Goofy carries the frog outside.

"I have him. . . . I have him. . . .
OOPS! I don't have him!" Goofy
yelps as the frog leaps right
toward . . . Daisy's painting!
SPLAT!

"You should look before
you leap!" Daisy says as the
paint splatters all around.

"Hey, there, little friend," Mickey says to the frog. "Slow down!"

But it is too late. The frog leaps out from behind Daisy's painting and heads straight toward . . . Mickey's bicycle. *BOING!*

He zooms down the road, holding tightly to the handlebars.

He is headed straight for a cliff.

"Oh, no!" Goofy shouts.

"Oh, Toodles!" yells Mickey. "We need you!"

"The lasso is the right tool for this job,"
says Mickey. "Thanks, Toodles!"
Mickey and Goofy carefully
pull the bicycle back from
the edge of the cliff.

"I think we should help our friend the frog find a nice, safe pond," Mickey says. "Then he can leap around without causing any trouble."

The frog jumps up and down in agreement. Then he hops away down the road with Mickey and Goofy following fast behind him.

The frog stops hopping in front of the pizzeria.

Just as Mickey reaches for him, the frog leaps right onto a . . . pizza pie. *SLOSH!*

"You should look before you leap!" shouts the man behind the counter.

The frog stops for a moment to clean himself off. Then he hops down Main Street, headed right toward Minnie and Pluto.

The frog takes a great big leap and lands right inside . . .
Minnie's goldfish bowl. *SPLASH!*

The big wave makes the goldfish fly right out. One more big
leap and the frog is out of the goldfish bowl, too.

"We need some help!" Goofy sighs.

"Oh, Toodles!" Mickey calls.

"The net is the right tool for this job," says Mickey. "Thanks, Toodles." Finally, the friends are able to catch up to the frog and place him safely in the net.

"He seems sad," Goofy says.

"I think you're right, Goofy," Mickey agrees.

Then Mickey looks ahead and sees something that makes him—and the frog—smile.

"I think we've found just the right place for you, froggie," Mickey says.

The friends walk quickly down the street toward the fountain.

Carefully, Mickey places the net on the ground and begins to lift the frog out.

But the frog is impatient.

Out he hops, headed straight for the . . .

. . . fountain.

The frog lands with a *SWOOSH!* right next to another frog.

A lady frog.

"*Ribbit, ribbit,*" he says.

"*Ribbit, ribbit,*" she replies.

"Maybe we didn't find a pond," says Mickey, "but we did find a good place for him to splash and leap."

"We've found the frog a friend, too," notices Minnie. "And they look very happy to see each other!"

"I think your goldfish is happy, too, Minnie!" adds Goofy.

Later, while Donald, Minnie, and Daisy make dinner, Mickey and Goofy get back to their game of chess.

"C'mon, Mickey," Goofy says. "Hurry up. You haven't made a move in a long time."

"I know. I know," replies Mickey. "I just want to make sure I look carefully before I leap!"

Tea Party Tantrum

After a fun sleepover, Emmie and Doc are finally awake and ready to eat breakfast.

"You two were up giggling awfully late last night," Dad chuckles.

Emmie yawns. "I know! I'm so tired."

Doc takes a bite of her cereal and realizes the mistake she's made. "Ack, I just put orange juice in my cereal by accident!"

"See what happens when you don't get enough sleep? It can be hard to think clearly the next day. Some people get cranky, and some people get . . . *spacey*!" teases Dad.

After Emmie goes home, Doc heads to her room. Her stethoscope begins to glow and her toys magically come to life.

"Hi, Doc!" Stuffy and Lambie shout. Susie Sunshine groans.

"Hi, guys! Who wants to have a tea party?" Doc asks.

"Me! Me!" Stuffy shouts, holding out his teacup. He pretends to slurp his tea very loudly. This makes Lambie giggle.

Susie Sunshine frowns and scrunches up her nose.

"Susie, would you like to join us?" says Doc.

"Nooooooo!" Susie screams as she kicks the table. "I don't want to!"

"Whoa!" Doc gasps. She's never seen Susie so cranky.

Lambie is confused. "But you love tea parties."

Susie crosses her arms. "Not today I don't!"

Doc is concerned. "Susie, you're not acting like yourself today."

"Yeah," agrees Stuffy, "you're usually so giggly and happy and . . . full of sunshine!"

"I think you need a checkup," Doc suggests.

"Awwww, I don't feel like having a checkup!" whines Susie.

"But Susie, I can't help you feel better until you've had one," Doc gently reminds her.

Susie finally agrees, so Doc brings her to the clinic.

Inside the waiting room, Hallie greets Susie. "Susie Sunshine! Just what we need to brighten our day. Give us a giggle, sugar!"

"I don't feel like giggling!" shouts Susie.

"Oh, my!" Hallie says.

"Susie isn't feeling like herself today," explains Doc.

"She didn't even want to play tea party today!" exclaims Stuffy.

"My, this is serious," remarks Hallie. "Let's see if Doc can put a smile back on your sweet face."

During her examination, Doc looks in Susie's ears and listens to her heartbeat. Everything seems to be fine.

When Susie yawns, Doc suggests she lie down.

"Huh, that's funny," Doc says.

"Nothing seems funny to me right now!" whimpers Susie.

"Susie, will you sit up for me again?" Doc requests.

"Ugh . . . okay," Susie groans, and props herself back up.

Doc thinks she's on to something. "Now lie back down, please."

"What, again?!" complains Susie.

Lambie tries to soothe her friend. "Susie, if Doc is asking you to do something, there's a good reason."

Even though she's cranky, Susie realizes that Doc is doing all she can to help her get better. She lies back down on the table.

Doc is close to a diagnosis. "Susie, when you lie down, don't your eyes usually close?"

"Yes!" wails Susie.

"That's it—I know what's wrong with you!" exclaims Doc. "Your eyes are stuck open."

Stuffy is confused. "But if Susie's eyes don't close when she lies down, how can she sleep?"

Susie gets weepy. "I guess I can't . . . *waaaah!*"

Lambie comforts Susie with a cuddle.

"I have a diagnosis," Doc announces. "Susie, you have a case of Eyes-wide-itis. That's why you can't sleep!"

"No wonder she's so cranky," Stuffy whispers to Lambie.
Susie's feelings are hurt. "I'M NOT CRANKY!"

Doc tells Susie a secret. "Last night I didn't get much sleep,
either, and this morning I was so tired I poured orange juice on
my cereal!"

This makes Susie giggle for the first time all day. "Really?"

"Really!" Doc assures her. "When
you don't get enough sleep, you can get
spacey . . . or cranky."

Susie looks at Doc. "Can you cure
Eyes-wide-itis, or am I going to be
cranky forever?"

"No, you won't be cranky forever," Doc promises. "Let's see what's happening with your eyes."

Doc uses her magnifying glass to get a closer look.

"I think I see something. Now I'm going to lightly touch your eyelid," Doc informs Susie. "That's strange. It feels really sticky."

Stuffy sniffs Susie. "Mmmmm, and she smells like pineapple!"

Doc thinks out loud. "Hmmm . . . Emmie and I had pineapple ice pops at our sleepover last night. Right before we played with Susie!"

"I know just what to do," Doc announces. "Wet wipes, please, Hallie."

"You got it, Doc!" Hallie says.

Doc gently wipes the sticky juice from Susie's eyelids.

Suddenly, Susie starts to blink!

"You did it—you unstuck my eyes!" But the more Susie blinks her eyes, the more she wants to keep them closed. Susie lets out a big yawn. "Aaaahhhh, I'm soooo, sooooo tired."

"It's time for you to get some shut-eye, sugar," whispers Hallie. "To feel healthy, full of energy, and back to your sunshiny self, you need plenty of sleep!"

Doc agrees. "Lots of rest is just what the doctor ordered."

Lambie and Stuffy start humming a lullaby to help Susie fall asleep. They gently cover her with a comfy blanket.

After several hours of sleep in Doc's clinic, Susie wakes up smiling and feeling refreshed.

"Wow, what a super sleep!" Susie cheerfully exclaims. "I feel so super-duper. Thanks, Doc!"

"You're welcome, Susie Sunshine!" says Doc.

"Now that I feel so good, I truly-duly want to have a tea party with you all," announces Susie.

The toys cheer. They're thrilled to see that Susie is back to her old self.

Doc closes up the clinic and heads to her house. Back in her bedroom, Doc and the toys continue their tea party.

"My dear party guests, I do hope you're all enjoying your tea," Doc says in a singsong voice.

Susie smiles as she slurps from her teacup. "Why, yes! This tea is simply scrump-dilly-icious!"

Doc is thrilled that Susie is feeling better. "I can't tell you how nice it is to see you so happy again and so . . ."

"Full of sunshine?" Susie giggles.

Finding Clover

Sofia has been busy lately—so busy she hasn't had much time to spend with Clover. So Clover decides to plan a whole day of fun for the two of them.

"It's going to be Clover-and-Sofia day!" he tells Robin and Mia.

The next day, a traveling magic show comes to the castle. A magician named Boswell makes a dove appear in his hand.

"*Wazza-wazoo!*" Boswell cries.

After that, he pulls a rabbit named Mr. Cuddles out of his hat. Then he puts Mr. Cuddles in a box and makes him disappear!

"I need a volunteer," Boswell announces.

James comes up onstage and steps into the box. With another *"Wazza-wazoo!"* Boswell opens the box, revealing Mr. Cuddles in James's arms!

Clover is impressed with Mr. Cuddles. "Must be nice being a star," he says.

After the show, Clover tells Sofia about Clover-and-Sofia day. Suddenly, Minimus crash-lands near them.

"What are you doing here?" Sofia asks him.

"We have Flying Derby practice, remember?" Minimus says.

Sofia gasps. She forgot all about that! "I'm sorry, Clover," she says. "I can't let the team down. I have to go!"

Clover can't believe it. What about Clover-and-Sofia day?

Just then, Mr. Cuddles hops out of Boswell's wagon and tells Clover he's quitting the magic show.

"But you're the star!" Clover exclaims. "Everyone loves you!"

"You want the job?" Mr. Cuddles says, hopping away. "It's yours."

Boswell comes out, searching for Mr. Cuddles.

"Sofia doesn't need me around," Clover tells Robin and Mia. "So it's time to join up with someone who does." He lets Boswell grab him and take him into the wagon.

The next morning, Sofia finds Clover's bed empty. The birds tell her what happened.

"But how could he just leave?" Sofia wonders, stunned.

"He said you didn't need him around anymore," Robin tells her.

Sofia can't believe it. She knows she has to find Clover. Robin and Mia offer to help her search.

As they're leaving the castle, Crackle the dragon lands and gallops toward them. "Where's my Clover?" she asks eagerly. When she hears what happened, she decides to go along on the search as well. "You never know when a dragon will come in handy," she says.

Sofia heads to the stable and asks Minimus to help. "I don't know which way the magic show went," she explains. "But I thought we could fly over the roads and try to spot them."

"Climb aboard, Princess," Minimus says.

Meanwhile, Clover is waiting to go onstage. "Ready for your first show, kid?" the dove asks.

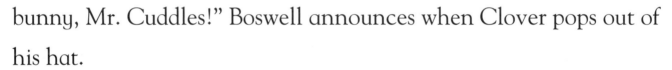

"Oh, yeah," Clover says. "Ready to be a star!"

"May I introduce my magic bunny, Mr. Cuddles!" Boswell announces when Clover pops out of his hat.

Clover doesn't mind what the magician calls him. He loves being the center of attention!

After the show, he's still excited. "If only Sofia could have seen the show," he says.

Sofia and the others search everywhere for Boswell's wagon. They find one that looks similar, but it belongs to a fortune-teller.

Madame Ubetcha offers to look for Clover in her crystal ball. "Crystal ball, don't be funny—help me find this girl's bunny."

Clover's picture appears! Sofia points to the bell tower behind him. "I've seen that tower before," she says. "It's in Somerset Village!"

It's almost time for another magic show. But Clover's heart isn't in it anymore. He misses Sofia—he wants to go home.

Boswell catches him trying to leave. "Where do you think you're going?" he exclaims, scooping Clover up. "I'm not about to have another bunny run out on me."

At the same time, Clover's friends finally find Boswell's wagon. Sofia opens the door and sees Clover in the magician's hat. Before she can rescue him, Boswell comes in. Sofia tries to explain that Clover is her pet rabbit. But Boswell won't let Clover go!

"I'll go to the castle!" Sofia exclaims. "I'll get the guards!"

Boswell isn't worried. "We leave Enchancia on a four-kingdom tour right after the show," he sneers. "So say good-bye, Mr. Cuddles!"

Sofia rushes to tell the others what happened. "We have to save Clover!" she exclaims.

Sofia comes up with a plan. She'll volunteer to go inside the magic box during the show. That way she'll end up holding the magic bunny—Clover.

But first she needs a disguise so Boswell won't recognize her. Suddenly, Madame Ubetcha appears, holding a cloak.

"I knew you'd need this," the fortune-teller announces.

Boswell doesn't realize Sofia is his volunteer. Once she's inside the box, Sofia sees that it has a fake back. "What are you doing here?" Clover exclaims when he recognizes her.

"Rescuing you," Sofia says. She sneaks herself and Clover out the back of the box.

Boswell is startled when he sees that the box is empty. He leaps into it just in time to see Sofia and Clover hopping off the wagon.

"Come back with my magic bunny!" he howls.

Sofia runs, holding Clover tightly. Boswell races after them.

"He's catching up!" Clover cries.

Sofia slides under a wagon, leaving Boswell behind.

But it's only for a moment. Boswell has long legs, and he soon draws close again. Then Sofia comes to a dead end.

"Yikes! Got any more moves, Princess?" Clover asks.

"Maybe one . . ." Sofia whistles, and Minimus lands in front of them. Sofia and Clover jump onto his back, and the flying horse takes off—but Boswell lunges forward and grabs Clover!

Boswell runs for his wagon. Suddenly, Crackle swoops down toward him.

"I'm coming for you, Clover!" she cries, sending a blast of purple flames at Boswell's feet.

The magician yelps and lets Clover go.

"I told you it would be handy having a dragon around!" Crackle exclaims as she grabs Clover and flies off.

Clover can hardly believe that all his friends came to rescue him. "Thanks, all of you," he says.

"Clover," Sofia says. "Next time, if you have a problem, promise you'll come talk to me before you go off and join a magic show."

Clover smiles. "You got it."

Sofia smiles back and hugs him tightly as they soar across the sky toward home.

Save Me, Smee!

"Blast it, Smee! I didn't sleep a wink all night," says Hook. "Captain Cuddly is missing! You know I can't go beddy-bye without my teddy bear."

Just then, Hook spots a teeny, tiny treasure chest. "Why, it's me first treasure chest from when I was just a wee little pirate."

There's a treasure map inside the chest!

"Captain, to get to the treasure, we have to go across Slippery Snake River and then pass through Crumble Canyon. Then X marks the spot at—*gulp!*—Skull Rock," says Smee. "Those are the most perilous places in all of Never Land."

"So what?" says Hook. "There's treasure and I want it."

179

"Be careful, Mr. Smee," says Jake. "You're heading for dangerous Slippery Snake River!"

Smee nods. "I'm afraid the captain's after treasure."

"We could follow in case there's any trouble," says Izzy.

"Oh, you sea pups are so kind," says Smee.

"Danger, schmanger," says Hook. "It's just a river." Hook jumps on the back of a slippery snake to cross.

BOING, BOING, SPLASH!

"Save me, Smee!" calls the captain.

"Oh dear, oh dear! Right away, Cap'n!"

BOING, BOING, SPLASH!

Smee falls into the river, too!

"We have to help Hook and Smee," says Jake.

Izzy makes a lasso and tosses it to Smee. "Mr. Smee, catch!" she calls.

Then Jake and the crew pull Smee and Hook to shore.

"Thank you, sea pups," whispers Smee.

"See? That wasn't dangerous at all," says Hook as he staggers to the shore and falls down.

"Oh, my," says Smee. "What do you say we go back to the *Jolly Roger* now, Cap'n? I'll make you a nice cup of tea."

"Never!" says Hook. "Crumble Canyon awaits!"

"Crackers! Hook and Smee are going across that narrow pass," says Skully.

"Be ready to lend a hand, crew," says Jake.

"See, Smee? This is a breeze," says Captain Hook. "I don't even know why they call it Crumble Canyon."

"Well, sir," says Smee, "it's because the sides of the canyon tend to . . . crumble," warns Smee.

"AIIEEEE!" yells Hook as the ground beneath him collapses. "Save me, Smee!" shouts Hook.

"I gotcha, Cap'n," says Smee.

"But who has *you?*" asks Hook.

"Oh! Oh!" shrieks Smee as he falls over the edge.

Skully swoops in and grabs Smee.

"I got you, Skully," calls Cubby.

"And I've got *you*," says Izzy.

"Come on, crew! Heave ho! Heave ho!" calls Jake.

Together, they hoist Hook and Smee to safety.

"Are you . . . okay . . . sir?" Smee pants.

"I'll be better when I have that treasure," says Hook.

"Are you sure you don't want to go home? I'll make hot chocolate with those little marshmallows you like so much."

"I do love those little marshmallows," says Hook, "but Skull Rock and the treasure await!"

"Hook can't go to Skull Rock," says Cubby. "It's way too dangerous."

"He'll never give up looking for that treasure," says Smee.

"Unless," says Izzy, "there is an even *better* treasure for him to find."

"Great idea, Iz," says Jake. "We can make a new treasure for Hook to find. Somewhere nice and safe."

"But we don't have any treasure," says Cubby.

"I know where there's a treasure that the cap'n will just love," says Smee.

"Skully, send word to Sharky and Bones to prepare the treasure," says Jake.

"Aye, aye, Jake!" says Skully.

"Cubby, can you make a new map?" Jake asks.

"Aye, aye, Jake!" says Cubby.

"Now to get Hook to take the bait," says Jake.

"Hey, Izzy," he says loudly enough for Hook to hear. "I can't believe we found a map to the most awesome treasure in all of Never Land!"

"Yeah. Lucky Captain Hook isn't around to take it," says Izzy.

"Ha! You can't fool the great Captain Hook. I'll be taking the map *and* the treasure," says Hook.

"Aw, coconuts," says Cubby, winking at Smee. "You tricked us again."

"We'll never find the awesome treasure now," says Skully.

"I don't believe me eyes. The treasure is aboard the *Jolly Roger*! The most awesome treasure in all of Never Land—right on me own ship," says Hook happily.

"Oh, is that so?" asks Smee innocently.

"Look alive," says Hook. "There be treasure aboard."

"X marks the spot," says Smee.

It's Captain Cuddly!

"Oh, my little cuddly wuddly! You are the greatest treasure in all of Never Land. Yes, you are," says Hook.

"He had a little rip," says Bones, "but I fixed him right up."

"Did you have an ouchy, Captain Cuddly?" asks Hook.

"Whew!" says Smee. "Now that we're home, I imagine you won't be needing any more rescuing today, Cap'n."

"Rescuing? What do you mean rescuing?" says Hook. "The great Captain Hook has never needed to be rescued. Isn't that right, Captain Cuddly?"

SPLASH! Hook accidentally knocks his bear overboard.

"Bear overboard!" yells Hook. He dives into the water . . .

. . . and finds his bear in the arms of the Tick Tock Croc!

"Save me, Smee! And Captain Cuddly, too!"

"Right away, Cap'n," Smee says as he jumps into the water.

THE
PIANO
LESSON

Henry Hugglemonster is bored with a capital B-O-R-E-D. There are only so many times a monster can toss a bright pink ball into the air and catch it all by himself. A good game of catch requires a partner—any partner at all. Like Daddo!

Except Daddo's in the kitchen juggling plates and a juicy slice of watermelon.

"*Ah ga goo!*" Henry's baby brother, Ivor, cheers.

"Daddo's busy cooking dinner," Henry sighs. "And Momma's getting ready for a piano lesson, so I can't bug her."

Then Henry remembers someone who is super fun to bug—his sister, Summer! He races up the stairs and barges into her room. Summer's twirling around on one webbed foot.

"No can do, Henry," Summer says before he can even ask. "I'm trying to beat the world record for monster pirouettes!"

"What's a pirouette?" Henry wonders.

Summer doesn't answer, she just keeps on spinning.

"So, it's just spinning?" Henry says. "Then I'll spin with you!"

Henry grabs his sister around the waist and starts to spin . . . and spin . . . and spin. Soon they topple to the floor.

"Henry, I almost had the record!" Summer says. "I was only off by 137 spins."

"Oh, sorry!" Henry apologizes.

"I know you're sorry, Henry, and I'm sorry I have to ask you to leave. But I have to pirouette—alone!" Summer says.

The only family member left to bug
is his big brother, Cobby. Henry knows
Cobby definitely won't be spin-rouetting!
He's busy inventing a new gadget.

"Hey, Cobby," Henry says excitedly.
"You want to play catch or something?"

"Sorry, little bro," Cobby replies.
"I have to finish this thing. Maybe later."

Henry tries to hide his disappointment.

"Sure, that's cool," he says.

Henry trudges out of Cobby's room.
Every single Hugglemonster is too busy
to play with him!

Just then, Henry hears a sound that
is music to his ears. *DING-DONG!*
It's the doorbell!

DING-DONG!

Gertie Glowmonster is standing at the front door, five minutes early for her piano lesson with Momma.

"Gertie's here to play with me!" Henry gushes. "I didn't even know she was coming. This is going to be ROARSOME!"

Henry runs back down the stairs and rushes to the front door.

"Hey, Gertie," says Henry. "It sounds like you're all ready to play!"

"I sure am, Henry!" Gertie replies.

"Roarsome!" Henry cheers. "I thought we could start with some catch, then play a little tag, and maybe build a fort."

"That would be great," says Gertie. "Except I'm not here to PLAY-play. I'm here to play the piano. I have a piano lesson with your Momma."

Daddo suggests that Gertie can stay to PLAY-play with Henry after her lesson. It all sounds perfect to Daddo, Momma, and Gertie. But it does not sound so perfect to Henry. He needs someone to play with now!

Gertie sits down on the piano bench and starts to tap the keys with her fingertips, showing Momma how good she has gotten by practicing for exactly 38 minutes every night, and twice on Sundays.

"Impressive!" Momma says.

Henry is not impressed. He is more bored than ever. He hides behind a chair and calls to Gertie. Then he sticks his fingers in his monster mouth, stretches his lips, and sticks out his tongue. Gertie giggles.

"Henry, what are you doing?" Momma asks.

"Um . . . making crazy faces to show Gertie how much fun she'll have when we play together?" Henry answers.

"Henry, we need to focus on our lesson now," Momma says seriously. "We'll call you when we're done, I promise."

"Okay, Momma," Henry sighs.

Henry agrees, but he isn't happy. The piano lesson is going to take forever! It feels like time is slowing down!

RAT-A-TAT!

Henry goes back outside. He slumps down on the front step and pats Beckett's furry head. That's when he has a great idea.

"If you can't beat 'em, join 'em," he says to Beckett as he runs off.

Henry drags a drum kit into the living room. Sticks in hand, he starts to bang a beat.

BAM BAM CRASH! RAT-A-TAT BOOM!

Gertie's graceful piano playing is now accompanied by lots of loud banging noises.

"Henry!" Momma calls loudly. "I can't teach Gertie with you banging on your drums. You can play with Gertie afterwards. Right now, I need you to be patient."

Patience is not one of Henry's strongest suits, but Hugglemonsters always find a way!

Henry sits on the stairs and tries to be patient. Then he hears Summer singing in her room. Maybe she's finished dancing! She's not.

"A true dancer never stops pirouetting," Summer sings. Then Summer gives her brother some advice. "When I'm looking for something to do, I usually dress up like a princess."

Henry doesn't think he'd make a good princess, but he is ready to try anything. He digs into Summer's dress-up box and pulls out a moustache and a top hat.

"Hey, I look like Gertie's dad," Henry chuckles when he looks in the mirror.

Henry decides to take his dress-up game to a new level. He runs outside and rings the front doorbell.

"Yeah, hello!" he calls in a fake, deep voice.

"Coming!" Momma calls as she opens the door.

"It's, ah . . . me, Gertie's dad!" Henry says. "I'm terribly awfully sorry, but I have to pick up my Gertie early! I mean, have her stop playing the piano so she can PLAY-play with her good friend, the very handsome and patient Henry Hugglemonster!"

"Oh, Henry!" Momma laughs. "What will you think of next? Gertie's lesson isn't finished yet. Patience, sweetie!"

"THIS MUST BE THE LONGEST PIANO LESSON EVER!" Henry wails.

"Hey, Henry!" Gertie says. "I can't wait to play with you, but I have exactly 13 minutes and 12 seconds left in my lesson. Then maybe we can have a snack together or something. Piano lessons make me hungry!"

Henry turns around and sees Daddo coming through the yard, his arms full of grocery bags and Ivor strapped on his back.

"Hey, kiddo," Daddo calls. "What's the matter?"

"It's just *really* hard to be patient!" Henry explains.

"Maybe you can find something fun to do until Gertie's finished?" Daddo suggests.

Henry follows Daddo and Ivor into the kitchen. He helps unpack the grocery bags full of supplies Daddo needs to finish his watermelon lasagna.

"Daddo, maybe while I'm being patient, I can bake something for Gertie!" Henry says.

Daddo thinks that's a roartastic idea. Henry knows that Gertie's favorite snack is ginger-and-baked-bean cookies.

"There's only one way to make them," says Daddo. "And it starts with a Huggle Juggle!"

While Daddo is busy juggling supplies, Cobby comes in with his new inventions—the Twixer Mixer and the Whipper Flipper!

Henry puts the ingredients into the Twixer Mixer.

Whirr! Swirl! Plop! Batter flies out of the mixing bowl and lands on Ivor's face.

"This is fun!" Henry cheers.

Henry rolls the dough into cookie shapes. Then Cobby pops them in the oven with the Whipper Flipper.

Eleven minutes and seven seconds later, Gertie comes into the kitchen.

"Henry! I finished my lesson, right on time!" she says cheerfully.

Henry looks up from the mixing bowl, surprised.

"Wow! That was fast!" Henry says. "Time really does zoom by when you're having fun. I forgot all about being patient!"

Gertie, Daddo, Momma, Cobby, Summer, and even Ivor laugh. And then they all sit down to share a snack of ginger-and-baked-bean cookies, followed by a roartastic game of catch!

Knight Time

"Who's ready for our big sleepover party?" squeals Doc.

"We are!" Lambie, Stuffy, Hallie, and Chilly shout together.

"What are we going to do at the party, Doc?" asks Chilly.

"Well, we're going to play games, tell stories, sleep in sleeping bags . . ."

"And have a pajama fashion show?" wonders Lambie.

"Sure," giggles Doc. "And I have a surprise special guest!"

"'Tis I, Sir Kirby! The bravest knight in all of McStuffins Kingdom," Sir Kirby announces as he bursts out of the toy castle to surprise his friends.

The toys all cheer, and Sir Kirby bows in appreciation.

"I am most delighted to be here, friends, as it is my first sleepover party ever."

"Oh, you'll love it, sugar!" says Hallie. "We're going to play all sorts of exciting games and get all snuggly in our sleeping bags."

"And then we'll turn off the lights and tell silly stories!" adds Stuffy. "Won't that be fun?"

Sir Kirby starts looking around the room nervously. "Uh, excuse me, did you say you'd be turning off the lights?"

"Yes, why?" asks Doc.

Doc notices a change in Kirby. He doesn't seem to be acting like himself. "Sir Kirby, you're breathing hard. Are you okay?"

"Oh, yes . . . yes! I'm perfectly fine," Kirby answers quickly. "Being brave is just so . . . uh, tiring."

"Well, I know something we can all do that's not tiring," Lambie says. "Let's play slumber party games!"

First the gang builds a tower of blocks . . .

. . . then it's time for the sleeping bag hopping race . . .

. . . and, finally, the slumber party fashion show!

The friends laugh and play until the wee hours of the night.

After the slumber party games, they all find spots on the floor to roll out their sleeping bags.

"Okay, everyone, it's time to snuggle up and turn off the lights," says Doc.

But as Doc walks toward the lamp on her bedside table, Sir Kirby dashes across the floor, jumps up on the table, and blocks the front of the lamp.

"My lady," cries Sir Kirby, "I must ask you not to turn off that light."

Doc is confused. "Well, why not?"

Sir Kirby pauses. "Well, you see, uh . . . I haven't done a check of the room. It's one of my most important knightly duties."

He hops off the table and begins to look carefully around Doc's room. "I need to make sure there are no dragons here. After all, I do need to keep fair Princess Lambie and Madame Hallie safe, don't I?"

"But I'm a dragon, and *I'm* here," Stuffy points out.

But Sir Kirby doesn't seem to hear him. He scurries to the other side of the bedroom. "Okay, no dragons or monsters here, either!"

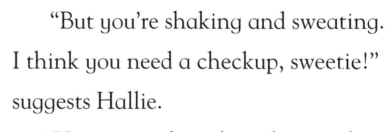

But when the lights accidentally get switched off, Sir Kirby screeches at the top of his lungs!

"Yiiiiiiiiiiiiiikes!"

When Doc turns the lights on, she sees Sir Kirby shivering in Lambie's arms. "Is everything all right?" she asks.

Sir Kirby pretends he's not nervous. "Why, of course! I was just . . . uh, just keeping Princess Lambie safe from any mean ogres."

"But you're shaking and sweating. I think you need a checkup, sweetie!" suggests Hallie.

"Hmmm . . . breathing heavy, fast heartbeat, and shaky and sweaty when the lights go off," notes Doc. "I have a diagnosis! You, Sir, have a severe case of the Dark Willies. It means you're afraid of the dark!"

"But, Lady McStuffins, how can I be a brave knight if I'm afraid?"

"Everyone's afraid of something," Doc tells him. "Even brave knights!"

Hallie has an idea. "You know, sugar, I bet you'd feel better if we told you what we're all afraid of."

"That's easy! I'm afraid of getting too hot, getting too cold, melting, getting lost under the bed, being mistaken for a dog toy . . . oh, and pickles!" announces Chilly.

"I'm afraid of hurting people's feelings," says Lambie, "and of polka dots. I do NOT like polka dots!"

Stuffy is next. "I'm not afraid of anything . . . er, except spiders!"

"And I'm afraid of thunder and lightning," admits Doc.

"That does make me feel better!" Sir Kirby smiles at his friends.

Doc is relieved. "I'm glad to hear that. Now, to know *how* to treat you, I need to know what caused your Dark Willies. Did you see something that scared you when the lights went out?"

Sir Kirby looks around Doc's bedroom. He points toward Doc's rocking chair, which has a jacket hanging from it. "When darkness fell, I saw something strange over there—like a scary monster!"

Doc, Lambie, and Stuffy inspect the chair.

"Nothing scary over here," Stuffy reports.

"Maybe this chair looks different in the dark," suggests Doc. Sir Kirby, will you be okay if we turn off the lights for just a second?"

Sir Kirby sighs. "If you must."

"Here, I'll hold your hand so you won't be scared," offers Lambie.

Chilly chimes in. "Me too!"

Doc prepares Sir Kirby. "Okay, get ready: I'm shutting off the light on the count of three—one, two, three!"

When the lights go out, Kirby looks toward the rocking chair.

"Aaack!" he screams. "It's the scary monster!"

Doc quickly switches on her flashlight. "No, it's not a monster—it's just the way the jacket looks on the chair when the lights are out. Nothing to be afraid of here!"

"By Jove, you're right!" exclaims Sir Kirby. "And yet, I still feel a bit strange."

Doc turns the lights back on and listens to Sir Kirby's heart through her stethoscope. "Your heart is beating kind of fast again. Your case of Dark Willies hasn't been totally cured."

Sir Kirby frowns. "Oh, dear."

Doc has an idea. "Let's use a night-light for our sleepover so it won't be so dark when we turn the lights out."

"I'm ready to give it the royal try!" agrees Sir Kirby.

With the night-light on, Sir Kirby feels calmer. "I feel better now that I see in the dark. Friends, toys, countrymen: Sir Kirby is back and ready for a sleepover party!"

"We knew you could do it, Sir Kirby!" cheers Lambie.

The friends get into their sleeping bags and get ready to tell bedtime stories. But as soon as he gets in bed, Sir Kirby falls fast asleep. "I guess the good knight just needed a night-light to say good night," Lambie says softly.

Doc whispers, "Nighty-night, brave knight!"

Make Way For
Miss Nettle

It's the end of the school day at Royal Prep. The clock tower chimes, its clockwork figures marching in circles, as Sofia and James head to the greenhouse for Royal Prep's after-school gardening club. On the way, they catch up with Prince Desmond.

"Hey, Desmond," James greets the other prince with a pat on the back.

Desmond jumps, startled. "James!" he exclaims. "You scared me."

"Sorry, Des," James says. "Just saying hi."

Flora, Fauna, and Merryweather flutter into the greenhouse and introduce the visiting enchanted gardening teacher. She's a fairy named Miss Nettle who was once their apprentice.

"Don't tire out your hands," Miss Nettle says as Sofia and the others applaud. "You'll be clapping much more once we get started."

227

Miss Nettle demonstrates how to grow a rising rose. It's so tall that it bursts out through the skylight!

Sofia sprinkles magic plant food on a bud. She grows a dancing daisy that sways and bobs around.

James grows a laughing lily. The flower blows a puff of magic pollen in his face, and he collapses with uncontrollable laughter.

"Don't worry, it wears off," Miss Nettle assures the kids.

Desmond does best of all. He grows an enormous singing sunflower. Even Miss Nettle is impressed!

Miss Nettle leaves the kids to practice their enchanted gardening. But she accidentally leaves her glove behind.

Sofia decides to return the glove. She arrives at the fairies' office just in time to see Miss Nettle magically grab the fairies' wands. Then Miss Nettle waves her own wand— and traps the fairies in a floating bubble.

Sofia waits until Miss Nettle flutters off, then rushes over to Flora, Fauna, and Merryweather. The fairies are glad to see her, but Sofia can't hear them through the bubble. So they act out what happened.

"Oh!" Sofia cries, finally getting it. "Miss Nettle wants to steal your spell book!"

The fairies nod. Then they start marching around. This time Sofia can't figure out what they're trying to say. But she's not giving up.

"I'm going to get you out of there, I promise!" she says.

She rushes back to tell the others what happened. "We have to find a way to rescue them!" she cries.

"Wait, why us?" Desmond asks nervously. He reminds the others that Professor Popov always stays late.

The kids rush to Popov for help. "Stand back, children," he announces. "I vill take care of zis!"

He finds Miss Nettle searching for the spell book. But as soon as he pirouettes up to her, she traps him in a bubble, too!

Sofia decides they have to find the spell book before Miss Nettle does.

"There must be a spell in there that can free the fairies," she tells the boys.

But where can the book be? Desmond suggests they check the library for a map of the school. "Then you can see every room," he says. "And every possible hiding place."

They study the map. Sofia notices the marching figures in the clock tower. "That's it!" she cries, remembering the way the fairies marched inside the bubble.

The clock tower is very tall, and there are no stairs. "The fairies don't need stairs," Desmond reminds the others.

What can they do? Sofia has an idea. "Can you grow a rising rose stalk big enough to reach the top of the tower?" she asks Desmond.

Desmond does it! The rising
rose grows up, up, up. . . .

Desmond is scared of heights,
but Sofia convinces him to climb the rose.
Once they all reach the top, they search for
the spell book. Suddenly, the clock chimes the
hour and the figures begin to move. . . .

"The spell book!" Sofia cries, pointing at one of the figures.

The kids chase the figure and grab the book. They did it!

"Bravo!" Miss Nettle says behind them. "Now hand it over."

Sofia clutches the book. "No!"

"We need it to free the fairies," James adds.

Miss Nettle offers them a deal. If they give her the book, she'll free the fairies.

Sofia isn't sure whether to trust her. Desmond nudges her. "I don't want to be put in a bubble," he whispers nervously.

"So do we have a deal?" Miss Nettle asks.

Sofia agrees. But as soon as Miss Nettle has the spell book, she flutters away. She tricked them! She's not planning to free the fairies until after she's the most powerful fairy in the world!

Sofia knows they have to stop her. They follow her to the greenhouse. Sofia notices the laughing lilies and remembers how they made James helpless with laughter.

"We can do the same thing to Miss Nettle!" she whispers to James and Desmond.

Desmond is the best enchanted gardener in the school. He's scared, but he agrees to grow more laughing lilies.

James creates a distraction by sending bouncing bluebells boinging toward Miss Nettle. Then Sofia and Desmond sneak up behind her.

Laughing lilies sprout all around the evil fairy.

"I'll get you!" Miss Nettle cries when she sees the kids.

Miss Nettle raises her wand, but it's too late. She doubles over, helpless with laughter. The spell book falls, and Sofia grabs it.

"Come on!" she yells.

The kids rush to the office and free the fairies.

"Thank you!" Flora exclaims.

"You're our heroes!" Fauna adds.

"Now where's Miss Nettle?" Merryweather grumbles.

The fairies and the kids find Miss Nettle in the greenhouse. She isn't laughing anymore. "I guess I'll just have to make one more extra-large bubble," she threatens, raising her wand.

Suddenly, Desmond leaps toward Miss Nettle. The bubble traps him—but he has Miss Nettle's wand in his hand!

"Way to go, Desmond!" James cries.

Without her wand, Miss Nettle can't cast any spells. The fairies order her to leave Royal Prep. "And never return!" Merryweather adds.

After Miss Nettle is gone, the fairies release Desmond.

"You were amazing!" Sofia tells him.

"I've never seen such bravery," Flora says.

Desmond blushes. He never knew he could be brave—until he had to be. Maybe he won't be so nervous from now on.

Sofia is happy for him. But something is bothering her. "I feel like we're forgetting something . . ." she muses.

Just then another bubble rolls past them.

"Professor Popov!" they all yell.

DADDO DAY CARE

Momma Hugglemonster is a busy monster. She gives piano lessons to the monster kids in the neighborhood, plays all kinds of instruments, and takes care of her family—Daddo, Cobby, Summer, Henry, and baby Ivor.

It's been a long time since Momma has had a chance to relax and unwind, but finally, the time has come. Momma is going on a weekend trip with her mom-monster friends!

"Tell me about it again!" Summer says.

"Well, we're getting our claw-nails painted, and our horns done, and I might even get my teeth sharpened," Momma gushes. "I don't know, that may be too much."

Henry is happy for his Momma, but he hopes they don't change her too much, because he loves her just the way she is.

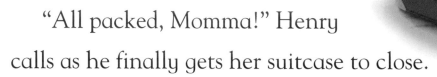

"All packed, Momma!" Henry calls as he finally gets her suitcase to close.

Momma heads toward the door. Her family gives her the biggest Hugglehugs and kisses.

"I hope I do okay on my own," Daddo whispers. "We usually take care of our Hugglefamily as a team! I'm not sure I can handle everything solo."

"Don't worry," Momma assures him. "Just use the list, like we always do."

Daddo and the Hugglekids wave good-bye until Momma is out of sight, then they go back into the house. Daddo looks at the list. It's longer than a Dugglemonster tunnel!

"Number one!" Daddo says as he consults the list. "My specialty: make breakfast!" Daddo begins to juggle whisks and bowls and ingredients in the air. Summer looks at the list.

"At the *same* time," she reads. "Put away the dishes, dress Ivor, set the table, pour juice, and sign Cobby's science-camp permission slip!"

"AT THE SAME TIME?" Daddo gasps.

Daddo flips a stack of monstercakes onto each plate.

"I can do this!" he cries as he sets the table with one hand, pours juice with the other, and then dresses Ivor in a flash. "Monstercakes for everyone!"

Luckily, no other Hugglemonster notices that one stack is short a monstercake, which is stuck to the kitchen ceiling.

"So what's next on the list?" Daddo asks. "Bring it on!"

"Um . . . I don't know," Henry admits. "I can't find the list."

Henry looks under the table. Cobby combs over the counter. Summer searches in the sink.

"It's missing," Summer agrees.

"Missing?" Daddo wails. "How am I going to keep everything straight WITHOUT THE LIST?"

"Easy," says Henry. "We're Hugglemonsters! We don't need a list to make it through the day!"

"All righty then!" Daddo agrees.

Daddo thinks about the things he and Momma do every Huggleday.

"Laundry!" Daddo shouts. "That is *always* on the list!"

The Hugglekids follow Daddo to the laundry room, and watch as he throws sheets and towels into the washing machine—along with the dirty plates from breakfast!

"Oops!" Daddo says, noticing his mistake.

"Don't forget my pink-as-a-pink-pony poncho!" Summer says.

Daddo takes out the plates, throws in the poncho, and then pours in the soap. That's when Henry notices his Huggleball jersey in the laundry pile.

"Isn't today my championship Huggleball game?" he asks.

"And I have my monster ballet class," Summer adds.

"Hugglefamily!" shouts Daddo. "We need teeth brushed, horns scrubbed, and bike wheels spinning in two minutes!"

"Um, Daddo," Henry interrupts. He points to the washing machine, which is bubbling over with pink soap suds.

Daddo stops the machine and pulls everything out. All the laundry is bright pink.

"Oh, that's not good!" Daddo moans.

Summer is thrilled to see that everything is pink—it's the best day ever! Her brother Cobby, however, does not feel the same way when he pulls a pair of his now-pink underwear from the pile.

"No time to fix it now, Huggletroops!" Daddo says. "We've got places to do and monsters to be! Wait, switch that!"

The Hugglemonsters rush out of the house. The kids jump in the sidecar while Daddo pedals furiously. Then he realizes that someone is missing.

"I left Ivor at home!" he cries.

A quick trip back to the house and the Hugglemonsters are on their way again.

First Daddo drops Cobby off at his science club meeting.

"Daddo!" Cobby calls.

"Science club is tomorrow!"

Then Daddo speeds Summer to her ballet class.

"Almost forgot these," he says, tossing an armful of Huggleballs into the dance studio.

Finally, Daddo races to the Huggleball field—and hands Henry a tutu!

"Daddo!" Henry groans.

"No need to thank me!" Daddo calls back. "It's all part of Daddo's job!"

That evening, after every monster has been picked up and with the list still nowhere in sight, chaos reigns at the Hugglemonster house.

"Where's my pink pony doll?" Summer whines.

"Ivor! Don't sit on me!" Cobby cries.

Daddo sighs and drags himself off the couch.

"BEDTIME!" he commands his Huggletroops. "I know *that's* on the list!"

The next morning, Henry finds Daddo and Cobby asleep in the kitchen.

"Hey, Daddo," Henry calls. "What are you doing?"

"I . . . I . . . I'm making a costume for Summer's dance recital!" Daddo says, startled. "And I'm fixing Cobby's rocket for his science club, which *is* today," Daddo continues.

"Daddo, you're doing a roarsome job," Henry says.

"I don't know. It's a big job for just one Daddo."

And that's when Henry realizes that Daddo shouldn't have to do it alone.

"We *all* need to take care of our house," Henry says. "We're Hugglemonsters, and Hugglemonsters *always* find a way!"

The Hugglemonsters don't
need a list, they need teamwork!
That's how Momma and Daddo
get things done every day. Daddo
rewashes all the pink laundry.
Summer picks up the stuff scattered on the floor.
Henry scrubs the walls. Cobby puts away his pink
underwear. Ivor and Beckett work together to clean
the floor. Soon the Hugglehouse is looking
good as new—just in the nick of time!

"Hellooooo!" Momma calls from the front door.

"Hello, Momma!" Daddo calls back happily.

Momma looks amazing! She feels like a new monster, too.

"Thanks, Daddo," she says. "I needed that."

"Well, I couldn't have done it without the whole Hugglefamily," Daddo admits.

Momma picks up Ivor and then pulls the list from his pajama pants. She looks curiously at her family.

"List?" Henry laughs. "We didn't need the list! We got along just fine!"

Blooming Bows

It's a busy day at Minnie's Bow-tique. Minnie and Daisy are getting ready for two special visitors.

"Daisy," says Minnie, "did you find the camera?"

"Not yet," replies Daisy. "But I know I have it here somewhere!"

"Here it is, Daisy," says Minnie.

"Thanks!" says Daisy. "Now I'll be able to get some good pictures of you and the twins."

Just then, Minnie hears giggling.

"Get ready!" she cries. "Here they come!"

"I'm Purple Posy!" says Melody.

"And I'm Rosie Posy!" says Millie.

Minnie greets her twin nieces while Daisy snaps pictures.

"Hold that pose, pretty posies!" cries Daisy.

"Oh!" says Minnie. "You both look simply adorable!"

As the girls twirl around to show off their costumes, some of the flower petals fall off.

Daisy snaps away as Cuckoo-Loca flies in for a closer look.

"All set for the Posy Pageant?" asks Cuckoo-Loca.

"We sure are, Cuckoo-Loca!" says Millie. "Come on, Melody, let's show them our posy prance dance!"

As the girls dance, more and more of the paper petals fall to the floor.

"Is that supposed to happen?" whispers
Cuckoo-Loca, pointing to all the petals
on the floor.

The girls sing:

"We can dance! We can sing!

On the first day of spring!"

"Oh, my," Minnie says.

The twins stare at all the petals on the floor.

"Uh-oh," says Melody. "I guess the glue wasn't dry."

"I'll say," says Cuckoo-Loca.

"Don't worry, girls," Minnie says. "We'll fix these right up."

"I've got the sticky-wicky goo-glue!" Daisy cries.

Minnie watches as Daisy glues the petals back on.

"Let's see, this pink one goes here, this purple one goes there. . . .

Wait . . . was that right?" asks Daisy.

"Daisy!" says Melody. "I'm Purple Posy! She's Rosie Posy!"

Minnie gives the twins a big hug. "There, there, now, girls," she says. "I'll figure something out."

"But how?" asks Melody. "It's a flower show, not a *bow* show!"

"Girls!" Minnie calls. "Follow me!" Grabbing an armful of fabric, Minnie leads the girls to the dressing room.

While Minnie cuts fabric and ties ribbons, the twins giggle excitedly. Daisy and Cuckoo-Loca can't wait to see what Minnie is creating.

Soon Minnie reappears and introduces the girls.

"Ladies and gentlebirds, introducing our favorite flowers: Rosie Posy and Purple Posy!"

"Pop-up posies!" cries Daisy. "And no glue needed!"

Minnie gathers the twins. "Come on, my little posies. It's showtime!"

"Hey, girls!" Daisy calls, holding up her camera. "Say *posies*!"

Millie and Melody wave good-bye as they run out the door.

"Wow, Minnie!" says Daisy, smiling at her friend. "Who knew you had such flower power?"

"It's like I always say, Daisy," says Minnie. "There's no business like *bow* business!"

No Place
Like Earth

"Hiya, everybody!" says Mickey. "Welcome to the Mickey Mouse Clubhouse Earth Day party. Professor Von Drake is our speaker."

"There he is now!" exclaims Minnie.

The professor begins, "Today, we celebrate the place we all call home—the planet Earth. Oh, excuse me. What do you have there, Mr. Toodles?"

What does Toodles have for the professor?

Yep, it's a globe.

"Aha! A globe is a map shaped like the Earth—the perfect Mouseketool for my talk. Thank you, Mr. Toodles," says the professor.

The professor gets serious. He says, "Earth needs our help. It is getting filled up with garbage. We must stop making so much garbage!"

"I know what you mean," says Minnie.

Minnie explains, "When I have a picnic, I don't use paper plates. I use real plates, and then I wash and dry them so I can use them again."

"That's right," says Daisy. "I never use paper napkins. I always use pretty cloth ones that I can wash and then use over and over again."

"Gawrsh," says Goofy. "I just lick my fingers!"

"Er, yes," says the professor. "Those are all good ways to cut back on trash. As I was saying—"

Now Clarabelle jumps in. "I don't use plastic or paper grocery bags! In my store, customers use canvas bags. Aren't they cute?"

"Thank you, Miss Clarabelle," says the professor. "Another way to make less trash is to share things. For example—"

"Toys!" yells Donald. "I always share my toys."

"Right," says Pete. "Donald lets me play with his lion sometimes, and I let him play with Clyde, my monkey."

"Very good," says the professor. "Sharing is an excellent way to reuse things. There are other ways to use things more than once, such as—"

"Oooh, oooh! I know!" It's Pete. He leaps onstage. "When my socks get old, I don't throw them away. I use them to make puppets—see?"

Poor Professor Von Drake faints.
"Oh, sorry," Pete says. "I guess I should wash the socks first, huh?"

Goofy splashes water on Professor Von Drake.

"Good job, Goofy!" says Mickey.

"Ach, water!" says the professor.

"The Earth is running out of clean

water. What I was going to say next is that—"

"We need to save water!" shouts Goofy. "I do that by taking shorter showers. I use a timer, and the bell rings after three minutes

Mickey explains, "I save water when I brush my teeth. First I wet the toothbrush; then I turn off the water while I brush."

"Woof!" barks Pluto.

"Right, boy! Pluto and Butch save water when they take a bath together!" says Mickey.

Minnie giggles. "And Figaro saves water by not taking *any* baths or showers!"

Professor Von Drake sighs. "The Earth is also running out of the fuels to make electricity. What I want to say about that is—"

Here comes Toodles again. What Mouseketool does Toodles have? That's right. It's a light switch!

"Very good, Mr. Toodles. As I was saying—"

283

"Turn out the lights!" shouts Goofy. "That saves electricity. I used to turn off the lights all the time. Now I know you should turn them out when you leave the room—not when you come in. A-hyuck!"

Professor Von Drake says, "Our Earth is also running out of the fuel that runs our cars, so what I must tell you is—"

"Carpool," says Minnie.

"Ride a bike," says Daisy. "Donald and I ride two at a time!"

"Or a skateboard," says Goofy.

"I always say there's nothing like using your own two feet—
or, in Pluto's case, your own *four* feet!" says Mickey.

Mickey shakes hands with Professor Von Drake. "Hot dog! You sure taught us a lot, Professor. Thanks!"

Professor Von Drake says, "You all taught me something, too. It seems like every day is Earth Day at the Mickey Mouse Clubhouse!"

"You betcha!" says Mickey. "Happy Earth Day, everyone!"

Engine Nine, Feelin' Fine!

"Lambie!" calls Doc McStuffins. "It's time to open the clinic."

She puts on her magic stethoscope and her toys spring to life.

"I don't know where Lambie is!" Stuffy says.

Suddenly, Doc's brother bursts into her room. He's pushing his toy fire engine, and Lambie is riding on top. In a flash, Doc's toys go stuffed!

"Will you play firefighter with me?" Donny asks.

"Maybe later, okay?" says Doc.

Doc, Lambie, and Stuffy head for the backyard.

"I'm going outside to play, Mom!" Doc calls.

"Okay, sweetie," Doc's mom says. "Just take care. It's a very hot day!"

"I will," Doc answers.

Doc opens the door to her clinic and flips over the welcome sign. "The Doc is in!" she says.

"Hi, Hallie!" says Doc. "Do we have any toys that need fixing?"

"No patients yet," answers Hallie. "My, my. It sure is hot today."

"It's even too hot to cuddle," adds Lambie.

Just then, Squeakers bounces through the door. "Squeak, squeak, squeeeeaaak!"

"What's he saying?" Stuffy asks.

"I don't know. I don't speak squeak," says Hallie.

Doc has an idea. "Squeakers, can you *show* us what's wrong?"

Squeakers leads Doc and the others to the backyard.

Donny says, "What's wrong with you, Engine Nine? I'll give you one more chance, but that's it." He pumps Lenny's siren and points Lenny's hose at a pretend fire, but nothing comes out! "Oh, no, you're broken!"

Donny sets Lenny on a pile of broken toys. "Sorry, Lenny," he says sadly. "You were an awesome toy. I'm going to miss you."

As soon as Donny walks away, Doc and the others run over to Lenny.

"What's wrong, Lenny?" asks Stuffy.

"I keep running out of water," Lenny says. "A fire truck that can't put out a fire isn't much good."

"Let's get you to the clinic, Lenny," Doc says. "It's time for a checkup."

Lenny is a little nervous. "What is a checkup, anyway?" he asks.

"It's when a doctor looks at you to make sure you're healthy," says Lambie.

Doc listens to Lenny's heartbeat.

"Sounds perfect," she says. "Lenny, has anything been bothering you lately?"

"Well, I've been feeling kind of tired and my head hurts sometimes," Lenny admits. "Mostly on really hot days."

Just then, there's a knock at the door! It's Doc's mom.

"Hurry," Doc says to her toys. "Go stuffed!"

"I brought you some water, sweetie," says Doc's mom. "I don't want you to get dehydrated."

"What's dehydrated?" Doc asks.

"If you don't drink enough water, especially on a hot day, you can feel sick."

"Dehydrated," repeats Doc. "That's it! Thanks, Mom."

"Lenny, you have Driedout-a-tosis!" announces Doc.

"What does *that* mean?" asks a frightened Lenny.

"It means dehydrated. Dehydrated is when you aren't drinking enough water," Doc explains. "Drinking water is important. But when it's hot outside, it's even *more* important!"

Doc puts down the glass of water in front of Lenny and says, "Be sure to drink all of it."

"Ah," says Lenny. "I feel better already!"

Hallie looks into the fire hose and asks, "Is this thing working now?"

Squirt!

"Yep, it sure as stuffin' is!" laughs Hallie.

Doc and the toys take Lenny back outside.

Donny is surprised to see Doc with his fire truck. "Engine Nine! What are you doing here?"

Lenny shoots a stream of water out of his hose.

"Awesome!" Donny shouts. "You're working again! I missed you, buddy."

"Now we can all play firefighter," says Doc.

"Help! Help!" shouts Doc. "We have to rescue Stuffy from the burning building!"

"Don't worry, Stuffy," yells Donny. "Engine Nine will save you!"

Donny points Lenny's hose at the pretend fire and water gushes out!

"Great job, Engine Nine!" says Donny.

"Thanks for playing with me, Doc," Donny says. "You're the best sister ever."

"I love hanging out with you, Donny," says Doc. "Almost as much as our toys do!"